In loving memory of
Peter Bartlett

Reprinted by permission of Lothrop, Lee & Shepard Books,
A Division of William Morrow & Co., Inc.

Printed in U.S.A.
First U.S. edition 1991   2 3 4 5 6 7 8 9 10

Library of Congress Cataloging in Publication Data
Ormerod, Jan. When we went to the zoo / Jan Ormerod.
p.   cm. Summary: Touring the zoo, two children pet, ride, and observe a variety of animals.
ISBN 0-188-09878-9.–ISBN 0-688-09879-7 (lib. bdg.) 1.Zoos—Juvenile literature.
2. Zoo animals—Juvenile literature. [1. Zoos. 2. Zoo animals.] I. Title.
QL76.076 1991 590'.74'4—dc20   90-6283 CIP AC

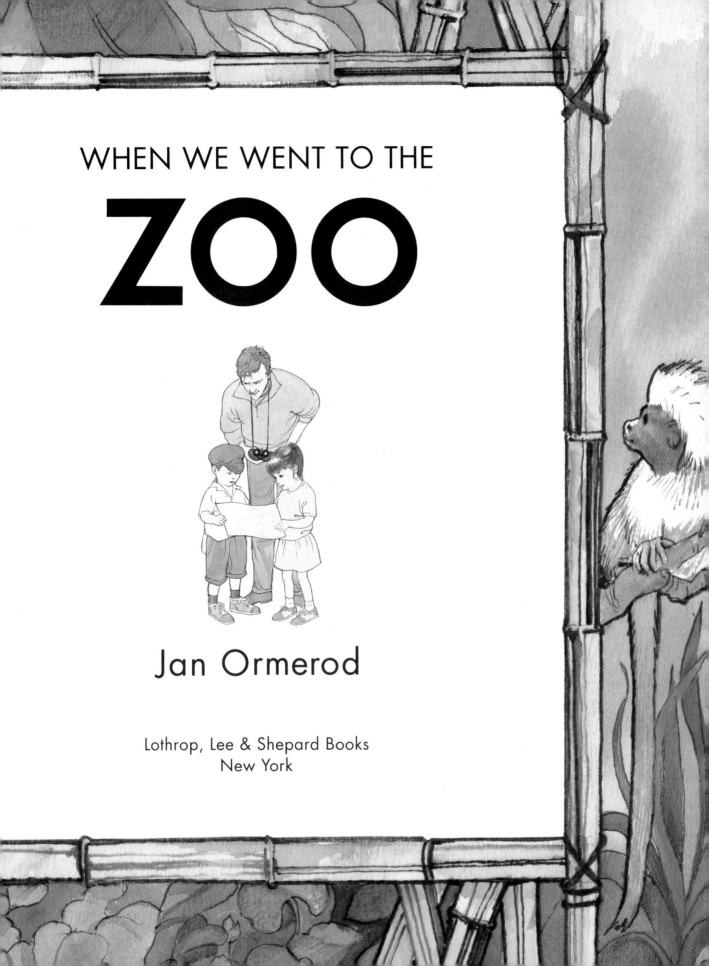

WHEN WE WENT TO THE
ZOO

Jan Ormerod

Lothrop, Lee & Shepard Books
New York

Ibex

Gibbons

Llama Rides

Pelicans

Elephants

Otters

Orangutans

Penguins

Sea Lions

Toucans

Emus

Sharks

Tropical Fish

Boa Constrictors

Goats

Rabbits

Lions

Camel Rides

Giraffes

Grizzly Bears

When we went to the zoo, we saw

a gibbon swing across Gibbon Island.

The pelican yawned

as we rode past.

We sang, "Hi-de-hi-de-ho,

the elephant is so slow."

We looked through glass

and saw an otter underwater.

We saw an orangutan carrying a

baby; another had a paper bag.

A penguin playing with a leaf

dived in and out of the water.

We watched the sea lions being fed.

We saw two big-beaked toucans

and some stripy emu chicks.

We saw a shark swimming in the dark,

and fish from a coral reef.

We touched a boa constrictor, a goat,

and a rabbit, which was very soft.

We spent ages looking at a

lion, a lioness, and their cubs.

We sang, "Bumpety, bumpety,

bump, we're on a camel's hump."

We saw the giraffes in their tall

giraffe house.

Just past the grizzly bear,

we spied the sparrows.

And in the end we liked

that best, spying the sparrows and their nest.